Bear's Adventure

BENEDICT BLATHWAYT

For Tom, Harry, Clare and Flora

This edition published in 2016 by
BC Books an imprint of Birlinn Ltd
West Newington House
10 Newington Road
Edinburgh EH9 1QS

www.birlinn.co.uk

in association with Tackle and Books
6-8 Main Street
Tobermory
Isle of Mull PA75 6NU

www.tackleandbooks.co.uk

Reprinted 2017

ISBN: 978 1 78027 365 5

First published in 1988 by Julia MacRae Books
New edition published by Tobermory Story, 2009

Printed and bound by Latimer Trend, Plymouth

This is Bear.

Bear loved to be beside the sea.

The children built sandcastles for him,

and sometimes they built boats.

But one evening they forgot all about him.

Bear watched the tide rise higher ...

and higher …

and he grew heavier and heavier …

until he sank down, down,
DOWN to the bottom of the sea.

The tide carried Bear along.

Round and round he went,

until BUMP! Bear was caught in a net.

The fishermen picked Bear up

and hung him out to dry.

Bear sat in the sun.

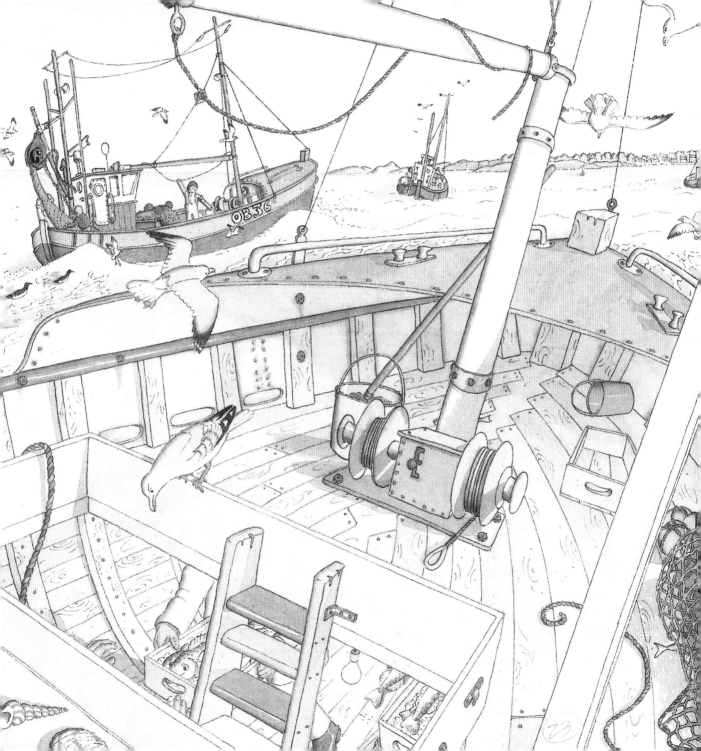

But when the boat tied up he was left all alone.

Not for long! A seagull picked up poor Bear.

Higher and higher
the seagull flew,

carrying Bear far, far away from home.

And then all the way back again.

At last the seagull let go of Bear,

right on top of a huge wave.

Bear was washed ashore.
He heard voices …

and then familiar arms
were holding him.
'Bear!' cried a happy voice.
Bear's adventure was over.